# The SANDMAN

# The SANDMAN

Ralph Fletcher

Illustrated by
Richard Cowdrey

HENRY HOLT AND COMPANY ∽ New York

**O**nce upon a time there was a man named Tor.
Tor was a tiny man, no more than a few inches high,
but he had a big problem.

He couldn't sleep. His head was jam-packed with thoughts, ideas, and worries. All night Tor lay in bed, longing for sleep, desperate for dreams.

He tried counting stars . . .

drinking warm milk . . .

taking hot baths . . .

but nothing worked.

One day while walking in the woods, Tor came
upon a place that smelled like smoke. With a start
he realized he had wandered near a dragon's nest.

Looking down, he saw a gleam of light at his feet.
A dragon's scale! He picked it up and hurried away.

Back home Tor examined the dragon scale. It was rounded on one side and jagged on the other. Tor took out a special tool and began to file down the sharp part. As he worked, a fine sand began to gather on his workbench.

Suddenly the door sprang open, and the wind blew sand into Tor's eyes. A great wave of sleepiness came over him. He couldn't keep his eyes open.

Hours later Tor awoke with a smile. He'd just had a most wonderful dream, and he'd never felt so rested. He blinked his eyes and tried to figure out what had happened.

"The sand from the dragon's scale!" he exclaimed. "It must have magical powers to put people to sleep!"

Tor wanted to help others who couldn't sleep, especially children. In his workshop he filed down the dragon scale to make more magical sand. He gathered it in a leather bag.

The next night Tor rode on a cart pulled by a mouse into a nearby home. Upstairs he found a boy lying in bed, his eyes wide open.

"Who are you?" the boy asked.

"I am the Sandman," Tor explained, sprinkling a bit of powdery sand over the boy's eyes.

"What do you—" the boy began, but his eyes closed before he could finish his sentence. He yawned, let out a sigh, and instantly fell into a deep sleep full of magnificent dreams.

And that's how the Sandman got started. Night after night he went from house to house, street to street, riding in his mouse-drawn cart, helping children fall asleep.

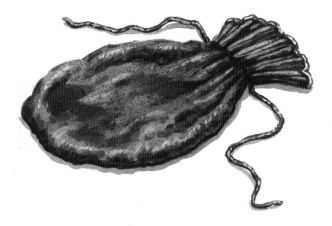

But there were so many children! In a few weeks the sand and the dragon scale were gone.

The Sandman knew what he had to do. He returned to the dragon's nest. He found a good place to hide and waited.

At first all was quiet. But then he felt a change in the air. A sudden gust of hot wind made his throat dry. He heard the terrible flapping of wings. Roaring, spewing great plumes of fire, the dragon returned.

The Sandman trembled, huddling in his hiding place. He kept still, barely breathing, while the dragon settled down for the night.

After a while the dragon opened its mouth, yawned, and stretched. A small scale popped off the dragon's belly and rolled into the dust.

The Sandman wanted to grab the scale right away, but he didn't dare. He waited until the dragon's red eyes closed. He waited until only smoke drifted from the dragon's great nostrils. He waited until its breaths came slow and easy. He waited a half hour more until he was absolutely certain the dragon was fast asleep.

Then, tiptoeing from his hiding place, he snatched the scale and raced back home.

Now you know how the Sandman lives. During the day he's in his workshop, grinding a dragon scale with a special metal tool, making a pile of magic sand. Since dragons live forever, there will never be a shortage of scales.

At bedtime he goes to work. The Sandman silently rides into your home, following secret pathways only a mouse would know. He tiptoes to your bed and reaches into his leather bag. With a quick flick of his wrist he sprinkles magic sand over your eyes.

Suddenly your eyes feel so heavy there is no possible way to keep them open. All those busy thoughts and worries disappear. Your breaths come nice and slow and easy. You give one huge stretch of your body . . .

like a dragon . . .

. . . and fall into a sound sleep.

A few hours later the Sandman rides home. He says good night to the mouse and climbs into his own bed. It makes him feel happy, giving others the gift of sleep. But some nights, even though he's tired, the Sandman has trouble falling asleep.

So he takes a little pinch of his special sand and sprinkles it over his own eyes—which always does the trick.

To Ethan and Liza,
who no way, unh-unh, never ever EVER
have trouble falling asleep!
—*R. F.*

To Hayla and Eliot
—*R. C.*

Henry Holt and Company, LLC
*Publishers since 1866*
175 Fifth Avenue
New York, New York 10010
www.HenryHoltKids.com

Library of Congress Cataloging-in-Publication Data
Fletcher, Ralph J.
The Sandman / Ralph Fletcher ; illustrated by Richard Cowdrey.—1st ed.
p.   cm.
Summary: A tiny little man discovers that sand made from a dragon's scale will send him to dreamland and
begins carrying this magical sand to children each night to give them the gift of sleep.
ISBN-13: 978-0-8050-7726-1 / ISBN-10: 0-8050-7726-X
[1. Sandman—Fiction. 2. Sleep—Fiction. 3. Dragons—Fiction.] I. Cowdrey, Richard, ill. II. Title.
PZ7.F634San 2008     [E]—dc22   2007002831

First Edition—2008 / Designed by Laurent Linn
The artist used acrylic paint on illustration board to create the illustrations for this book.
Printed in China on acid-free paper. ∞

1  3  5  7  9  10  8  6  4  2